I CAN
READ ABOUT
GHOSTS

Written by Erica Frost

Illustrated by Frank Brugos

Troll Associates

Andrew was a ghost. He was a very little ghost. He was much too small to haunt the old castle on Whispering Hill.

So, when the ghost council met, Andrew told them that he did not want such a *big* job.

"It's too scary," he explained. "There's no one to talk to, and I'm afraid of the dark."

The other ghosts laughed.
The Great Ghost rose in the air and
pointed his long, white arm at
Andrew.

"Afraid of the dark?"
he asked in a
loud voice.

"Go back to the castle!"
said the Great Ghost.

"Do you want to be a
ghostling forever?"

Andrew hated to be called
a ghostling. A ghostling
was a baby!
A ghostling was a
beginner who
couldn't do
anything
right!

The moon was high as Andrew flew toward the castle.
He sighed very softly and his voice floated on the
night air in a ghostly sort of way. "OOOOOOOOOOOOOooooooooooo."
Andrew liked the sound of it. He decided to try again.

The castle was dark and spooky. No one had lived in it for over 100 years. Spider webs stretched across every dark corner. Bats flew in and out of broken windows. There was even a suit of rusty armor.

Andrew floated around from room to room. Then suddenly,

something soft and furry
ran past him. A small gray
mouse squeaked and vanished
into the darkness.

Andrew hid inside the suit of armor. He was afraid of mice. He was afraid of everything! Alone in the dark, he cried.

"Boo HOOOOOOOOOoooooooo."

In the village,
people locked
their doors.
"It's the ghost,"
they said.
"Listen! It's
the ghost of
Whispering
Hill."

Later, Andrew came out of his hiding place and floated around. He flew around the castle sighing and moaning. He didn't want to be a ghostling. He didn't want to be a baby. He wanted to be big and brave, like the Great Ghost!

Booo

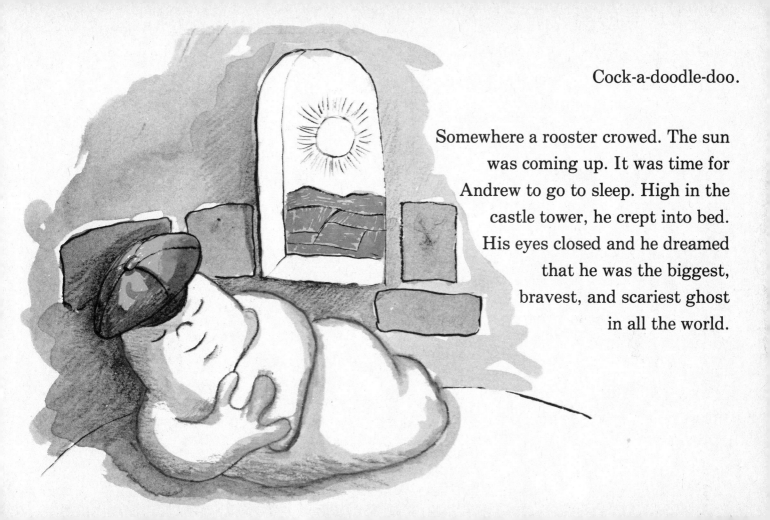

Cock-a-doodle-doo.

Somewhere a rooster crowed. The sun
was coming up. It was time for
Andrew to go to sleep. High in the
castle tower, he crept into bed.
His eyes closed and he dreamed
that he was the biggest,
bravest, and scariest ghost
in all the world.

Suddenly, strange voices woke him up.
A man, a woman, and two children were
standing at the bottom of the stairs.

Men hurried in and out carrying furniture. Chairs and couches.
Lamps and tables. Bright rugs and cushions. Pictures to hang
on the walls. A family was coming to live in the castle!

The days that followed were filled with dusting,
mopping and scrubbing. The windows were fixed.
The mouse holes were plastered. The
walls were painted, and vases
were filled with flowers.

Andrew watched it all. He saw the dark and dreary castle become a bright and cheerful home. He sighed with relief when the last little mouse was swept out the door.

"AAAAAAAAAAAAAAHHHHHHHHHHHHHHH!" sighed Andrew.

Everybody stopped what they were doing. "Did you hear anything?" asked Mrs. Thornapple. "I believe I did," said Mr. Thornapple. "I believe I did." "A ghost!" shouted the Thornapple children. "It sounded like a ghost!"

AAAAAAHHHH

"Don't be silly," said the parents.

"Who ever heard of a ghost in this day and age."

But the children did not answer. They were looking for the ghost.

Poor Andrew!

He was
hiding
in the
corner
of a
closet.
He didn't want to be found.

Suddenly, the closet door was thrown wide open.

"OOOOOOOOOOOOOOOOOOOOOoooooooooo," moaned Andrew.

"A ghost!" shouted the children.
"A ghost! A ghost! A ghost!"

Andrew almost fainted.

Mr. and Mrs. Thornapple hurried up the stairs
to see what the fuss was about.
"How wonderful," they beamed
when they saw Andrew.
"Our castle is
haunted!"

The children introduced themselves.

"I'm Kevin."

"I'm Laurie."

"I bet you can't scare me," said Laurie.

"BOO!" said Andrew.

"Not
like
that,"
said
Laurie.

"Like this," said Kevin. The children ran around the room, flapping their arms and moaning. Andrew was quite surprised.

"You're not a very
good ghost,"
said Laurie.

Andrew hung his head.
"I'm just beginning,"
he said.
"It's not easy,
you know.
It takes
a lot of
practice."

That night, when everyone was asleep, Andrew sat alone in the dark.
"I'll never be a real ghost," he thought. "Never, ever, ever."
   Just then, he heard a sound. A man with a flashlight
and a big bag crept softly into the house.

The burglar picked up a pair of silver candlesticks and put them into his big bag. Andrew wanted to run away. He wanted to hide in the closet, but he remembered the words of the Great Ghost:

Do you want to be a ghostling forever?

Andrew took a deep breath. He floated
up in the air and raised his arms
above his head. "OOOOOOOOoooooooo,"
he cried in his deepest
and scariest voice.

When the burglar saw Andrew, he dropped his flashlight and
the bag with the candlesticks in it. "H-h-help!" he cried.
"A g-g-g-ghost!" Then he ran out the door so fast that
he was gone before Andrew could blink his eyes.

The lights went on, and the Thornapples came running down the stairs. When they saw the candlesticks and the open door and the happy smile on Andrew's face, they realized what had happened.

"You scared him away!" said Kevin. "You were terrific," said Laurie.

"Congratulations," said Mr. and Mrs. Thornapple.

Andrew didn't say anything. He just stood there and smiled. He was thinking how nice it would be at the next meeting of the ghost council. What a good day that would be!